THIS WALKER BOOK BELONGS TO:

_____

_____

_____

First published 1983 by Julia MacRae Books
Published 1992 by Walker Books Ltd
87 Vauxhall Walk, London SE11 5HJ

This edition published 2019

2 4 6 8 10 9 7 5 3 1

© 1983 Brun Ltd

The right of Anthony Browne to be identified as author/illustrator of this work has been
asserted by him in accordance with the Copyright, Designs and Patents Act 1988

This book has been typeset in Palatino

Printed in China

British Library Cataloguing in Publication Data:
a catalogue record for this book is available from the British Library

ISBN 978-1-4063-9514-3

www.walker.co.uk

ANTHONY BROWNE
GORILLA

WALKER BOOKS
AND SUBSIDIARIES
LONDON • BOSTON • SYDNEY • AUCKLAND

Hannah loved gorillas. She read books about gorillas,
she watched gorillas on television and she drew pictures
of gorillas. But she had never seen a real gorilla.

Her father didn't have time to take her to see one at
the zoo. He didn't have time for anything.

He went to work every day before Hannah went to school and in the evening he worked at home.

When Hannah asked him a question, he would say, "Not now. I'm busy. Maybe tomorrow."

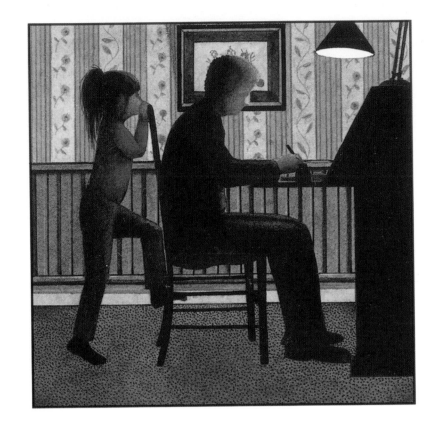

But the next day he was always too busy.

"Not now. Maybe at the weekend," he would say.

But at the weekend he was always too tired.

They never did anything together.

The night before her birthday, Hannah went to bed tingling
with excitement – she had asked her father for a gorilla!

In the middle of the night, Hannah woke up and saw a
very small parcel at the foot of the bed. It *was* a gorilla,
but it was just a toy.

Hannah threw the gorilla into a corner with her
other toys and went back to sleep.
In the night something amazing happened.

Hannah was frightened. "Don't be frightened, Hannah," said
the gorilla, "I won't hurt you. I just wondered if you'd like
to go to the zoo."

The gorilla had such a nice smile that Hannah wasn't afraid.
"I'd love to," she said.

They both crept downstairs and Hannah put on her coat.

The gorilla put on her father's hat and coat. "A perfect fit,"
he whispered.

They opened the front door and went outside.

"Come on then, Hannah," said the gorilla and he gently lifted her up. Then they were off, swinging through the trees towards the zoo.

When they arrived at the zoo it was closed and there was
a high wall all around. "Never mind," said the gorilla,
"up and over!"

They went straight to the primates. Hannah was thrilled.
So many gorillas!

The gorilla took Hannah to see the orang-utan and a chimpanzee.
She thought they were beautiful. But sad.

"What would you like to do now?" the gorilla asked.

"I'd love to go to the cinema," said Hannah. So they did.

Afterwards they walked down the street together.

"That was wonderful," said Hannah, "but I'm hungry now."

"OK," said the gorilla, "we'll eat."

"Time for home?" asked the gorilla.

Hannah nodded, a bit sleepily.

They danced on the lawn. Hannah had never been so happy.

"You'd better go in now, Hannah," said the gorilla. "See you tomorrow."

"Really?" asked Hannah.

The gorilla nodded and smiled.

The next morning Hannah woke up and saw the toy gorilla. She smiled.

Hannah rushed downstairs to tell her father what had happened.
"Happy birthday, love," he said. "Do you want to go to the zoo?"
Hannah looked at him.

She was very happy.